Oh Boy, Boston!

OTHER YEARLING BOOKS ABOUT THE POLK STREET KIDS YOU WILL ENJOY:

THE BEAST IN MS. ROONEY'S ROOM
FISH FACE
THE CANDY CORN CONTEST
DECEMBER SECRETS
IN THE DINOSAUR'S PAW
THE VALENTINE STAR
LAZY LIONS, LUCKY LAMBS
SNAGGLE DOODLES
PURPLE CLIMBING DAYS
SAY "CHEESE"
SUNNY-SIDE UP
PICKLE PUSS
BEAST AND THE HALLOWEEN HORROR
EMILY ARROW PROMISES TO DO BETTER THIS YEAR
MONSTER RABBIT RUNS AMUCK!
WAKE UP, EMILY, IT'S MOTHER'S DAY

Plus the Polk Street Specials

WRITE UP A STORM WITH THE POLK STREET SCHOOL
COUNT YOUR MONEY WITH THE POLK STREET SCHOOL
TURKEY TROUBLE
THE POSTCARD PEST
SHOW TIME AT THE POLK STREET SCHOOL
LOOK OUT, WASHINGTON, D.C.!
GREEN THUMBS, EVERYONE
PET PARADE
NEXT STOP, NEW YORK CITY!

YEARLING BOOKS are designed especially to entertain and enlighten young people. Patricia Reilly Giff, consultant to this series, received her bachelor's degree from Marymount College and a master's degree in history from St. John's University. She holds a Professional Diploma in reading and a Doctorate of Humane Letters from Hofstra University. She was a teacher and reading consultant for many years, and is the author of numerous books for young readers.

A Polk Street Special

Oh Boy, Boston!

Patricia Reilly Giff

Illustrated by Blanche Sims

A Yearling Book

Published by
Bantam Doubleday Dell Books for Young Readers
a division of
Bantam Doubleday Dell Publishing Group, Inc.
1540 Broadway
New York, New York 10036

ISBN: 0-440-41365-6
Printed in the United States of America
October 1997
10 9 8 7 6 5 4 3 2 1
CWO

Oh boy . . .

Conor James Giff

February 18, 1997

To welcome you with love and joy

Oh Boy, Boston!

A Special Report by Dawn Tiffanie Bosco

Long ago a bunch of people left England. They didn't want to be British anymore. They sailed to America. Some built homes in Boston, Massachusetts.

They wanted to go to their own churches. They wanted to be farmers or fishermen, or have their own shops.

They didn't want the British to tell them what to do!

But the king of England said America

belonged to England. He sent British soldiers to America.

The British were strong. They were much stronger than the colonists in Boston. They had fancy red coats. They had shiny guns.

The colonists had old brown clothes. They didn't have a lot of guns.

The only thing they could do was stick together like glue.

They would tell each other when the British were coming. They'd hide. Then they could jump out.

They'd surprise the British.

In Boston, they knew the British were coming.

Were the British coming by land? Or were they coming by boat?

A man stood in the tower of Old North Church.

Paul Revere told him to put up one

lantern if the British were coming by land, and two if they were coming by sea.

The man saw the ships.

He told Paul Revere.

Paul rode all over to tell the colonists.

Everyone was ready.

The Americans won.

That's how we became a country . . . by sticking together.

And it all started in Boston.

Chapter 1

Richard "Beast" Best raced up the aisle.

He slid over bits and pieces of shiny paper. A red spider. A green dragon. A loopy orange worm.

Half the class was working on kites.

He was in the other half.

Sherri Dent looked up. "You're going to be in trouble if Ms. Rooney comes back."

He kept sliding. "Yeow."

He grabbed on to Sherri's desk.

"Thanks a lot, Beast," Sherri said. "You just ruined my tiger tooth kite. It was the best one I ever made in my life."

Ms. Rooney popped back into the room. She had scissors in one hand. She had a jar of paste in the other.

She frowned at Beast. "Kite people in front," she said. "Play people in back."

Sherri raised her hand. "Beast finished his kite. Now he's a play person."

"He's the star," said Emily. "He has to say a million things."

"Just what I'm saying," said Sherri. "He's supposed to be practicing."

"Tattletale," said Beast.

"He's stepping on my dreadful dragon kite," said Linda Lorca.

"Double tattletale," he told Linda.

He went back along the aisle.

He sat down at the science table. The play people were working on the story of Paul Revere.

Too bad. He was Paul Revere.

Too bad he had finished his fat frog kite early. A green one with yellow spots.

No more kite group.

Instead he was in the play. It was all about a poem.

The poem had been written by a guy named Longfellow. Some name! The poem was called "Paul Revere's Ride." Beast had to tell the colonists the British were coming. They were going to fight.

And he had to tell which way the British were coming . . . by land or by sea.

He never could remember.

All he knew was he had Dawn Bosco for a wife. He had sixteen kids.

Nobody was going to see the children. But they were going to see plenty of Dawn Bosco.

She wasn't afraid. She loved being a star.

Beast rolled up a paper missile. He shot it across the table. He'd never let anyone know he was afraid.

"Let's start over," Timothy Barbiero said. "This play is about Americans in the olden days. The colonists."

"Everyone knows that." Dawn smacked her lips together. "I'm going to wear lipstick when we do this. Cherry red."

"The British soldiers are strong," said Timothy. "There's a pile of them. The colonists have to be brave. They have to stick together. They have to fight to be free from the king."

"I'm a British soldier." Matthew

jumped on Beast's back. "I'm going to fight you."

Ms. Rooney stood up. "And I am going to give everyone two minutes to get back to your seats."

Beast circled around Timothy. He hopped over a bunch of kite sticks. He slammed down into his seat.

Ms. Rooney pushed her hair back. "Put your kites on the science table. We have to take good care of them."

"I would," said Sherri, "if it weren't for Beast. He stepped on mine. There's a hole in my tiger's ear."

"There's a hole in my ear too," said Matthew.

Beast heard a snuffle.

He looked up.

Jill Simon looked as if she was going to cry. "I can't fly a kite," she whispered. "I don't even know how to begin."

"You have to run," Beast whispered back. "Run like the wind. Pull the string, and zippo. . . ."

Jill was crying now. "I can't run either."

"Don't worry," he said. "So what if the kite crashes?"

His kite was gonzo. It had sailed away somewhere.

Ms. Rooney leaned forward. "I'm not going to say another word. But those kites are very important."

"I thought so," said Dawn.

"But—" Beast began.

"I hope you put yours away carefully," Ms. Rooney said.

More trouble.

Beast sank down in his seat.

He wished he could sail away somewhere.

Gonzo.

Just like his kite.

Chapter 2

It was after school on Monday. Beast was in Matthew's backyard. Dawn was there too.

They were working on the play again.

Beast galloped across the lawn. "The British are coming," he yelled at the top of his lungs.

Dawn tugged at her hair. "Wrong. All wrong."

Beast stopped galloping.

"You have to look up at the tower of Old North Church first," she said. "Someone's going to put a light up for you to see. If the British sneak up on land—"

"I know," Beast said. "Two lanterns."

Dawn slapped her forehead. "One. O-N-E. And two if they sneak up by sea."

"I know," he said again.

Dawn shook her head. "You'll be watching the tower. You'll ride around telling everyone where the British are."

"Don't you think I know that?" He galloped across the driveway.

He stopped. "What should I say?"

Matthew started to laugh.

Dawn shook her head. "You're going to ruin this whole play."

"Don't worry," Matthew said. "We'll stick together. We'll—"

"Why did Ms. Rooney give you this part?" Dawn cut in. "Why did she let you in the play at all?"

Beast looked in the garage window. He didn't want them to think he had tears in his eyes.

They'd think he was just like Jill Simon.

He put two fingers in his mouth. He stretched his lips to see how far they'd go.

Matthew dived on top of him. "I'm a British troop," he said. "Take that, Paul Revere."

They rolled over.

"You American colonists will never be free," Matthew said.

Beast tried to catch his breath.

Someone was calling now. "Beast? Matthew?"

Emily Arrow was coming up the driveway.

"News," she called. "Great news."

Beast sat up.

"It's about the kites," she said. "It's about the play."

"Ms. Rooney's going to forget the whole thing?" Beast asked.

He felt great. He felt wonderful.

He dived on Matthew's head.

But Emily was shaking her head. "That's not the news."

"How come you know all this news?" Dawn asked.

"Ms. Rooney is calling the parents," Emily said.

Beast sat back. He wondered what Ms. Rooney would say.

"We're all going to Boston," said Emily. "We're going to fly kites in a field.

We're going to do the play for a whole school there."

A whole school. Beast swallowed.

"Cherry red lipstick," said Dawn. "I'll need blush too."

"I bet we're going on a bus," Matthew said. "A big huge—"

"You bet wrong," said Emily. "We're going in cars. Some of the mothers are driving."

"I hope I get to go in Dawn's car," Matthew said.

Beast nodded. Dawn had everything. She probably had a TV in her car. Maybe even a refrigerator with soda and stuff to eat.

At that moment Matthew's grandfather drove up the driveway.

Matthew grinned. "Just as long as we don't have to go in Pop's van."

Beast nodded. He watched Pop open his van door.

The van was a mess. It needed paint and it rattled.

The stuffing was coming out of the seats.

Pop grinned at them. "I have a great piece of news," he said. "Guess where I'm taking you this weekend?"

Chapter 3

It was Friday. Beast was standing in Matthew's driveway.

Jill was there too. She was hiding behind the car with her kite and her bag.

She was ready to cry.

It was because of Kissie Poo, his dog.

Kissie had come with him to say good-bye.

They were leaving for Boston.

"I'm terrified of dogs," Jill said.

"She's got only three teeth," said Beast. Poor dog. No hair on her tail. Bulgy eyes and buck teeth.

Matthew came out of the house. He was holding his kite. "Pop is having coffee," he said. "It'll take ten hours."

"Great kite," Beast said.

It was white with black zigzags.

"It's a mystery monster kite," Matthew said.

Beast and Matthew chased each other around the house.

Jill leaned on the hood of the van. "I'm afraid that dog will get mean."

"Don't worry," Beast said. "She'll go home."

Dawn came up the driveway. She was carrying two purses and two bags.

"How is all that supposed to fit?" Beast asked.

"We're going to do a lot of stuff," Dawn said. "I need these. Shirts and sweaters and books . . ."

Beast thought about the trip.

Ms. Rooney had talked about it every minute for days.

They were going to see Paul Revere's house. He knew that.

They were going to sleep in a school.

He knew that too.

He swallowed. They were going to do the play for everyone in the school.

Pop came out of the house. "I feel like a million dollars," he said.

The van door was open. Inside, it smelled of cough drops.

"All aboard," Pop said.

Beast grabbed a seat next to the window. He could feel stuffing. It was poking into his back.

"Front seat," Dawn yelled. "Called it."

"It's a nice roomy van." Jill twirled one of her four braids. "Thank you for taking us, Mr. Jackson."

Matthew threw his bag in. It was a huge red backpack. It said YAHOO across the front.

He threw his kite in too. He sank down next to the other window.

Jill looked as if she would cry again. "I forgot to tell you," she said. "I get car-sick."

Beast looked at Matthew. "Yucks. Throw-up . . ."

"All over the nice roomy van," said Matthew.

"Maybe I should sit in front," Jill said.

Dawn stared out the window.

"I hope I don't throw up over—"

"Let her sit in the front seat," said Matthew.

Dawn shook her head. "I'm trying to

count license plates from different places."

Jill sniffed. "You could count in the backseat."

Dawn sniffed too. "You can't see, sitting between Beast and Matthew."

Pop pulled on his mustache. "Maybe Jill should sit next to a window."

Beast looked out at the street. He made believe he couldn't hear.

Matthew was looking down at his shoes.

"I guess I'll have to sit in the middle," Jill said.

Jill shoved her suitcase in the back. It landed on Beast's foot.

It probably weighed as much as Jill, he thought.

She plumped herself down between them.

She held her kite in front of her.

The kite had a fat bunny face on it. It looked awful.

The sticks were crooked. It had a pound of glue on it.

It would never fly.

"Everybody ready?" Pop asked.

Beast thought about it. Suddenly he remembered something.

He had forgotten his suitcase.

He opened his mouth.

"All right," said Pop. "We'd better hurry. They'll be waiting at the school for us."

Beast thought about the things in his bag. His pajamas. Clean shirts. His Paul Revere costume.

He opened his mouth again.

Pop backed the van down the driveway. "We're going to meet up at the school," he said. "The three cars. Then we'll follow each other to Boston."

Beast closed his mouth. He had a wonderful idea.

The best idea of his life.

He'd ask someone else to be Paul Revere.

Timothy Barbiero or Noah Green. Wayne O'Brien. Alex Walker.

There were plenty of people who could do this.

He sat back.

He felt like a million dollars.

Jill was taking up a ton of room. Her kite stick was jabbing into his arm.

Dawn's stuff was all over the place too.

So what?

He wouldn't have to think about "one if by land," or Paul Revere, or the whole play.

Pop parked in back of the other cars.

Beast could see Ms. Rooney's Ford.

"Look," said Matthew. "Mrs. Green has a green Dodge."

Ms. Rooney was out of her car. "Stay on I-95," she said. "All the way."

She waved to Beast and the rest of the kids. "Just think," she said. "Tomorrow you'll see Old North Church."

Beast nodded. He wondered what was so hot about Old North Church.

"I bet you don't know what that is," Dawn said.

"One if by land," Matthew whispered.

The tower, Beast thought. The man had put up the lanterns there.

"Everyone have their kites?" Ms. Rooney asked.

Beast swallowed.

The cars pulled out. They headed for the highway.

Beast didn't have time to think about a kite.

He could see something under the seat. It looked like . . . He leaned forward.

It was a tail without any hair.

It was Kissie Poo.

Chapter 4

The trip was taking forever.

They were never going to get to Boston.

They'd stopped about four times to go to the bathroom.

Now Jill was holding a paper bag over her face.

The whole van smelled like throw-up.

And then there was Kissie Poo.

Beast had pointed her out to Matthew.

It was a good thing they had a secret language.

It was easy. *Issie-kay* meant Kissie. *Oopay* meant Poo.

"What are we going to do?" Beast asked.

Matthew looked serious. "Keep her idden-hay."

Before Beast could answer, Dawn was yelling. "It's a Connecticut license plate. Blue and white. Called it."

And Pop was talking about Boston. "You have to take a good look at that place," he said. "The colonists started to fight the British there. They were ready to be free."

"There's the Freedom Trail in Boston," Dawn said.

"Good girl," said Pop.

Dawn nodded back at them.

"Knows the whole orld-way," said Matthew.

"New York license plate," Jill yelled through her paper bag. "White and blue and red."

Beast jerked his chin toward Kissie's tail. "I hope she isn't hungry," he whispered to Matthew.

"I hope she doesn't have to go to the athroom-bay," Matthew whispered back.

Dawn sat up straight. "I'm going to tell you all about Boston," she said.

"Yucks," said Beast.

Dawn had a book in her hand. "The Freedom Trail is marked. A piece of the street is painted red. You can just follow it along."

Just then Noah Green's car passed them. Inside they could see Derrick taking a picture of the traffic.

Noah and Sherri were eating apples.

Beast felt his mouth water.

"Too bad we don't have a snack," Matthew said.

"Of course we have a snack," Pop said. "Look in the glove compartment there," he told Dawn. "See what you can find."

Beast stuck his head up. The glove compartment was filled with junk. Old maps. Bits of paper. Half a roll of mint candies with most of the paper missing.

"Told you," Pop said to Dawn. "Pass them out. One to a customer."

Everyone took one.

It tasted strange, Beast thought. Not like mint. More like . . .

"Best cough drops in the world," Pop said.

"Now, about the Freedom Trail," said Dawn. "It begins at a park. It's called Boston Common."

Beast could see Kissie Poo's tail wiggling. He wondered if she'd like a cough drop.

He took his out of his mouth. He wiped it on his shirt.

He put it down under the seat.

Kissie just sniffed at it.

He guessed Kissie didn't like cough drops either.

"Cows used to hang out on Boston Common. It was in the olden days," Dawn said. "Every family could keep one there. They kept sheep there too."

"Moo," said Matthew.

"Baaa," said Beast.

"Great cough drops," said Pop.

Dawn looked up. "You know what else? British troops used to march up and down on Boston Common."

"Left—right—eft-lay," said Matthew.

Underneath the seat, Kissie Poo started to snore.

Beast began to make drumming sounds to cover up the noise.

"I'm really going to throw up this time," Jill said.

"Faneuil Hall," said Dawn. "Say it like 'fan-yul.' It's a great big building. Americans made speeches there."

She looked back to see if they were listening. "Next to it is a market," she said. "You can buy things. Cut-up fruit, and soda, and cake, and sausages, and . . ."

Beast's mouth was watering.

Kissie Poo was still snoring.

Jill was gagging.

Pop was singing, "Boston is Beantown. . . ."

"Hey," said Matthew. "Look. Up ahead."

"What?" Beast asked.

And then he saw them too. Buildings bunched together. A plane coming in for a landing. And a huge gas tank painted with great splashes of color.

He stood up to get a better look.

He stood on Kissie Poo's tail.

She gave him a sharp nip on the ankle.

"Yeow," he yelled.

"So what's going on back there?" Pop asked. "The Revolutionary War?"

"What's that?" Beast asked.

Dawn shook her head. "You don't even know that?"

"It was the war with Paul Revere in it," Jill said. "The colonists fighting the British . . . trying to get the United States going."

Beast didn't have to answer.

Jill was throwing up in her paper bag again.

Chapter 5

Everyone was getting out of the cars. Ms. Rooney and some of the kids up in front. People in Noah Green's car.

Everyone was piling out of Pop's van too.

Beast was in a hurry.

He had to pick someone to be Paul Revere.

Timothy. He was a smart kid.

He'd be an okay Paul Revere.

Matthew grabbed his arm. "Issie-kay," he said.

Beast stopped. How could he have forgotten? What could he do with that poor dog?

If Jill saw her, she'd be yelling all over the place.

"Good old Yahoo backpack," Matthew said. He turned it upside down.

A pile of Dubble Bubble gum came out. So did underwear and pajamas with paint and a hole in the knee.

At least Matthew had pajamas, Beast thought.

"A couple of other things in there," Matthew said. "A shirt. Stuff like that. They'll make a nice pillow for Kissie."

Jill looked back. "Hurry," she said. "You'll get lost."

Beast stuck his head out the window. "We're coming. Matthew is just—"

"Here comes the tricky part." Beast reached for Kissie.

Kissie gave him a nip on his finger.

That Kissie was the testiest dog in the world.

"What about the athroom-bay?" Matthew said.

Beast sat back. "I never thought of that."

He took a deep breath. He pulled Kissie out. "We need some string," he told Matthew. "We've got to put it on her collar for a leash."

Matthew nodded. "We'll walk her on the other side of the van."

Beast looked around. Jill's kite string was lying on the floor.

"Enough for the British army," said Matthew.

Beast broke off a piece. He threaded it through Kissie's collar.

Then they were out the door. They kept their heads down.

They sneaked around the back of Pop's van.

"Hey, where are you?" Jill called.

Beast stuck his head up. "Coming."

"You'd better come fast. Ms. Rooney is counting noses."

"Good girl, Kissie." Beast put her gently into the backpack.

"It's a good thing she loves to sleep," he told Matthew. "That's all she does all day."

Matthew tucked Kissie's tail in, and they followed the class.

Everyone was heading for a park.

Ms. Rooney waved her hand around. "We're here at last," she said. "Boston is known for its parks. There are so many that—"

"They're called the Emerald Necklace," said Dawn. "All green . . ."

YA HO

"With willow trees," said Emily.

"And this is the Public Garden," said Ms. Rooney. "The rest is called Boston Common."

Beast sank down on the grass. He reached into the backpack. He could feel Kissie's wiry hair.

The cough drop was stuck to it.

"I can't wait to see the ducklings," said Jill.

Beast frowned. Kissie liked to chase birds. She had never caught one, but . . .

Ms. Rooney pointed. "Look. On Charles Street, facing the park."

Emily Arrow smiled. "Jack, Kack, Lack, Mack, Nack, Ouack . . ."

Beast opened his mouth. "Pack and Quack," he said slowly.

He could see the ducks. It looked as if they were heading toward the park. But they weren't moving. They were bronze ducks. Ducks that looked like . . . something in a book Gram had read to him. He just couldn't remember.

Ms. Rooney smiled. "There are real ducks too. But these are the ducks from the book *Make Way for Ducklings*."

"I loved that story," Jill said. "I'm not one bit afraid of ducks."

Ms. Rooney was talking again. "Look at the swan boats," she said. "People have been riding in them for more than a hundred years."

"The same people?" Matthew said. He gave Beast a little shove.

A man walked by. He was selling hats with three corners.

"Just like the colonists," Matthew told Beast. "I'll buy us each one. I have a ton of birthday money."

Beast plopped a hat on his head. "Cool," he said. "Thanks."

They stood in line for a swan boat ride.

Beast made sure he could sit near Timothy.

He waited for a moment, feeling the boat slide through the water.

Then he leaned over. "Listen, Tim," he said. "I left my Paul Revere costume home."

Timothy shook his head. "Too bad."

Beast nodded. "How would you like to be Paul instead?"

"Me?" Timothy asked. "What would I do about a costume?"

Beast tried to think. "Maybe I could get a costume somehow."

"Good," Timothy said. "Then you can be Paul Revere."

Chapter 6

Beast's feet were tired. So were his legs. They had walked all over the place.

First they had seen the State House. It had a round gold top.

Next they had marched down School Street.

"Look at the Boston Latin School," Ms. Rooney had said. "It's the first public school we had in this country."

Then they had gone to a cemetery. It

was called the Old Granary Burying Ground.

It was filled with people from the days of the colonists.

"Beast will love to see this," Ms. Rooney said. "Paul Revere is buried here."

Beast swallowed.

He looked at the old stones. Then he looked at Noah.

He hoped Noah loved seeing it.

He was going to ask Noah next.

They started to walk again.

"There's Milk Street," Ms. Rooney said. She was nodding. "Benjamin Franklin was born there."

Beast looked down at the backpack. He could see a bit of Kissie's head.

He wondered how much she weighed.

It felt like a thousand pounds.

He moved the backpack from one arm to the other.

Timothy had stopped on the corner.

Beast didn't look at Timothy. Timothy wasn't such a great friend after all.

Noah was probably much better.

Noah would make a great Paul Revere.

Beast wondered if he could sit on the curb for a minute. "My feet are falling off," he told Matthew.

"Mine too," Matthew said.

Everyone else was walking. They were on their way to Quincy Market.

Ms. Rooney and Pop turned the corner first. Then Dawn.

Beast sank down on the curb with Noah and Matthew.

"I can't walk one more inch," said Matthew.

Noah nodded.

"Listen, Noah," Beast said. "About Paul Revere."

Noah nodded again. "We're going to see his house this weekend. We're going to see Old North Church too."

Beast looked down at the curb. He crossed his fingers. "Paul was a neat guy," he said.

"I think so too," said Matthew.

"How about—" Beast began.

Noah was looking down the street. "We have to get going," he said. "We have to catch up. Get something to eat at Quincy Market."

Beast and Matthew stood up too.

Noah began to run.

"Wait," Beast called. "How would you like to be Paul Revere?"

Noah looked back. "No thanks. I'd be dead."

"No," Beast said. "I mean in the play. I mean instead of me."

Noah smiled. "You'll make a great Paul Revere. Besides, I don't have time to learn all that."

Noah turned the corner. "Thanks anyway," he called.

"Want me to carry Kissie for a while?" Matthew asked.

Matthew was a good friend, Beast thought. A great friend.

He handed him the backpack.

It was probably a thousand miles to Quincy Market.

But he didn't mind.

He didn't even mind about Noah.

He had another idea.

A perfect idea.

He'd just switch with Matthew.

It would be the easiest thing in the world. He could be a British troop.

Matthew could be Paul Revere.

Chapter 7

"Next stop," said Ms. Rooney, "Quincy Market. Plenty to see. Plenty to hear. Plenty to eat."

Jill rolled her eyes. "I'm starved," she told Beast.

"Me too," Beast said. He felt a little worried. Kissie would be starved too.

He looked down. He made sure she was covered.

Ms. Rooney was walking ahead of

them with Pop. "A kite festival," she was saying. "The children will be so excited."

Beast moved closer.

He could see that Jill was moving closer too.

"I've signed up the class," said Ms. Rooney. "It's the kite festival in Franklin Park."

Beast sighed. He had no kite.

Jill was sighing too. "Now what am I going to do?" she said.

Just then they reached the market. Beast could hear music. He could smell wonderful things.

So could Kissie.

"I can't fly a kite," Jill was saying.

Beast kept his hand on Kissie's head. Any minute she'd be out of the backpack. She'd head straight for the sausages and peppers.

They wandered down the aisle. A million people were walking around. All of them were eating.

A clown stood at one end. He pulled handkerchiefs out of his pocket. Red silk ones. Ones with blue polka dots.

He saw Beast. He pulled out a chicken made of rubber.

"Cluck," Beast said.

"I'm too worried to laugh," said Jill.

Kissie was wiggling around now.

Beast stopped for a bag of french fries. He squirted ketchup on them.

He dropped a couple into the backpack for Kissie.

Kissie loved french fries.

Someone was handing out balloons. You had to hold on to them.

"Let go for one second," Matthew said, "and it's gonzo."

They looked up at the ceiling high above them. Dozens of balloons were floating around.

Jill caught up with them. She had french fries and ketchup too. "I'm heading for lemonade next, and maybe an ice pop."

Beast could feel the backpack wiggling.

At the same time Jill's eyes grew bigger. She opened her mouth.

She started to yell. "Something alive . . . ," she began. "A thing with a pink tail . . ."

Kissie jumped. She sailed up the aisle away from them.

Her ears were up. Her tail was straight as a string.

"It's the sausages." Beast took off after her. He held his three-cornered hat on with one hand.

"What?" Jill kept asking. "What?"

"My dog," Beast yelled over his shoulder.

The three of them began to run.

Matthew followed Beast.

Jill went in the opposite direction.

Beast saw an opening behind a counter. He dashed that way.

He could feel his heart pounding. "Wait, Kissie," he yelled.

But she was gone.

And so were Matthew and Jill.

Beast went up one aisle and down another. Who would take a dog with a bald tail and three teeth?

And then he heard a yelp.

He stopped. It was Kissie.

Down the aisle, he saw Jill. She had wrestled Kissie to the floor.

Kissie had a sausage in her mouth.

"Help," Jill said. One of her braids had

come undone. Her hair hung down over her face.

Beast picked Kissie up.

Matthew helped Jill up.

"You saved him," Beast said.

"We have to stick together like glue," she said. "Just like the colonists."

She shook her head. "That was the scariest thing I ever did."

Jill had turned out to be a great friend, Beast thought. The best, after Matthew.

Beast gave Kissie a hug. Then he closed his eyes.

For a moment he had forgotten about Paul Revere and the colonists. He had forgotten about doing the play for the whole school.

He looked at Matthew.

It was almost time to ask Matthew to be Paul Revere.

Chapter 8

"I never slept in a school before," said Jill.

"Me neither," said Beast.

They were sitting in the gym of Freedom School.

Beast looked at Matthew. "Jill was right," he said. "We have to stick together."

"Like glue," said Matthew.

"Isn't it great?" Ms. Rooney said

from up in front. "Sleeping bags in the gym."

"The best," said Pop.

A man was standing with Ms. Rooney. He had a beard and a red tie.

"Welcome to Freedom School," he said. "We have pizza for dinner . . . and pancakes for breakfast."

Beast tapped Matthew on the shoulder. He took a breath.

He said it all at once.

"I can't be Paul Revere," he whispered.

"How about Alex?" Matthew whispered back. "Or maybe Jason?"

"I don't think . . . ," Beast began, and stopped. "How about you?"

Matthew started to laugh. Then he stopped too. He began to shake his head.

Beast didn't give him a chance. "We have to stick—"

"I know," Matthew said. He was beginning to look worried.

No, worse. He looked scared. "I can't—"

"You'd be a great Paul Revere," Beast said. "The greatest. And you'd save my life."

"Pancakes tomorrow," said the principal of Freedom School. "Then the kite festival. And we'll see Paul Revere's house and Old North Church afterward."

Matthew was still staring at him. "How can I remember all that stuff?" he asked.

He looked like Jill Simon.

He looked as if he'd cry any minute.

"I can help you," Beast said. "We'll work on it. 'One if by land . . . two if by sea.' "

"But—"

"You're my best friend, Matthew," he said. "I'm counting on you."

Matthew ran his tongue over his lips. "All right," he said. "I'll do it."

A cafeteria lady was rolling in trays of food. There were glasses of juice and slices of pizza.

It all smelled wonderful.

"Matthew," Beast said, "I feel like a million dollars."

But next to him, Jill looked sad. "I don't know what I'm going to do," she said.

Beast didn't look at Matthew again. Matthew might look sad too.

Beast didn't feel too happy either.

What would Ms. Rooney say when she found out he had no kite?

What would she say if she knew Kissie was here?

What would she say if she knew he didn't even have a suitcase?

One good thing. He didn't have to tell her about that.

He just couldn't get pizza on his shirt. He'd wear the same stuff tomorrow.

No one would know.

No one would care.

Ms. Rooney was still talking to the man with the beard. The principal of Freedom School.

Beast stepped over a couple of sleeping bags.

He took a breath. "I have to tell you something," he said to Ms. Rooney.

Ms. Rooney smiled. "Here's our Paul Revere," she told the principal.

"Well . . . ," Beast said.

The principal smiled. "I can't wait to see this play," he told them.

Then he went to help the lady with the pizza.

"I don't have a kite here," Beast told Ms. Rooney in a rush. "I have a dog."

"A dog?" she said. "In the school?" She shook her head. "How could that be?"

Beast kept nodding. "It's Kissie Poo. She hid in Pop's van and then it was too late."

Ms. Rooney looked around. "But where?"

Beast pointed toward Matthew and Jill. "Don't worry. We're all taking care of her. We're feeding her. She's having a great time."

"I guess . . ." Ms. Rooney ran her fingers through her hair. "One small dog doesn't take up that much room."

"No," said Beast.

"Don't let her out of your sight."

"I won't," Beast said. "I'm going right back there now. I'm—"

"Wait a minute," Ms. Rooney said. "What about your kite?"

Beast swallowed. "It flew away. Gonzo."

"Good grief. What next?" Ms. Rooney shook her head.

The cafeteria lady stopped in front of them. She held out a tray of pizza.

Beast took a big slice.

He remembered to take a napkin.

He took another piece for Kissie, and water. "Thanks," he said over his shoulder.

Ms. Rooney was the best.

He tripped on one of the sleeping bags.

He dropped the pizza all over his shirt.

Chapter 9

It was morning.

Everyone was jumping into the cars again.

Beast stopped to wipe pancake syrup off his shirt.

He wiped pizza stains off too.

He put Kissie in the backpack and slid into the backseat of Pop's van.

Jill was looking at the floor. "I don't

even have enough string," she said. "What happened to my string?"

Beast shook his head. "Sorry. I used it for Kissie's leash."

"Don't worry," Jill said. "I can't fly it anyway."

"Everyone ready?" Pop asked. "We're off to fly kites . . . to see Old North Church . . ."

"And old Paul Revere." Beast gave Matthew a little tap.

It was a sunny day, a windy day. A perfect kite-flying day.

And there must have been a million people in the park.

Kites were in the air. Some were on the ground. Yellow ones and red ones. Ones with stripes and stars and polka dots.

Jill was dragging her beautiful bunny kite in back of her.

Beast could hear music. Someone was singing, "Up, up, and away . . ."

A man was selling pinwheels that spun around. He was selling hot dogs too.

Jill leaned over the Yahoo backpack.

She put one finger out to pet Kissie.

"Maybe I'm not afraid of dogs anymore," she said.

Beast took Kissie out of the backpack.

She blinked in the sunlight.

"Fresh air is good for her," Beast said.

He wound the string on her collar around his wrist.

Then he took Jill's kite. He straightened the four sticks. He scraped off some of the glue.

"You have to put the string around something," he said. "You have to keep it out of the way."

Jill was nodding.

"Otherwise you'll fall all over it."

"I did fall," she said. "The other day."

"Listen," Beast said. He picked up a twig.

He wrapped the string around it.

"You can fly this thing," he said. "I'll help you."

For a moment they watched everyone running. Kites were sailing up.

Sherri's tiger tooth.

Linda's dreadful dragon.

"Come on, Jill," he said. "We'll stick together like glue."

Jill was frowning. "I'll never get it up."

"Take the string," he told her. "This kite's not bad."

He crossed his fingers. "The bunny looks okay."

Jill started to laugh. "It doesn't even look like a bunny. It looks like—"

Beast took a breath. "A bad beast," he said. "Like me."

Kissie was asleep in his arms.

He put her carefully on the ground.

He put the kite on the ground too.

"I'll stand here," he said. "I'll help it up."

Jill was shaking her head.

"Just run," he told her. "Hold your arm up, the string in your hand."

"Well . . . ," she said.

"Run like the wind," he told her. "Go."

Jill took off.

Beast had to smile.

She was a terrible runner . . . with a terrible kite.

He gave the kite a push.

Kissie opened one eye and growled at it.

And then the kite was up.

Up and sailing.

It didn't look like a bunny or a beast.

The blue and white looked like part of the sky.

Jill had stopped running.

Her head was back.

She was watching, smiling.

And then Beast saw Matthew.

Matthew was sitting next to a tree.

He hadn't even begun to fly his mystery monster kite.

He looked worried.

Beast looked up at Jill's kite. He didn't want to think about Matthew.

He knew why Matthew was worried.

Chapter 10

They had seen Paul Revere's house. Kind of skinny, Beast thought. And not enough room for sixteen children.

Eight with his first wife. Eight with his second.

Now they were standing on the Paul Revere Mall—all of Ms. Rooney's class.

"Where are the stores?" Dawn asked. "What kind of a mall is this?"

Ms. Rooney smiled. "Not the same

kind of mall. This kind means an open space."

Beast gave Matthew a tap. "I like the other kind better."

He reached down and touched Kissie's head.

Kissie was back in the backpack. She was taking a nap.

Jill shook her head. "I was never so tired in my life," she said. "But I'm a kite flyer now."

Matthew was a kite flyer too.

At the last minute Beast had talked him into sailing his mystery monster kite.

It had sailed high.

Matthew's three-cornered hat had flown off. It had sailed high too.

The kite had crashed into a tree. So had Linda Lorca's.

Ms. Rooney had smiled. "That's what happens with kites sometimes. We'll just have to make new ones."

Beast and Matthew had chased after the hat.

Right now they were standing at the far end of the mall. They could see a gate.

Beast pointed. "There's Old North Church. It's the oldest church in Boston."

They stood there looking at the tower.

"A man was up there," Beast said. "He could see the British boats. He put . . ."

Beast closed his eyes for a second. He tried to remember.

Then he started again. "The man put two lanterns up."

They walked closer to the church.

"The colonists were ready," Beast said.

Jill nodded. "They stuck together like glue." She patted Kissie on the head.

Ms. Rooney was nodding. "I told you, Beast," she said. "You'll make a great Paul Revere."

"That's what I want to tell you . . . ," he began.

Ms. Rooney put her hand on his shoulder. "You're a great kid too," she said. "I like the way you took care of your dog."

"And flew my kite," Jill said.

Ms. Rooney went into the church. "This is going to be a terrific play."

Beast stood by the gate.

Matthew didn't feel great.

He knew that.

He knew something else too. It wasn't fair to ask Matthew to be Paul Revere.

Jill was watching him. "A great Paul

Revere," she said. "It'll be like sailing a kite."

"Up, up, and away," he said. "Maybe I'll crash into a tree."

Dawn was standing behind him. "And maybe you won't."

She put her hands on her hips. "I can't wait to put on that lipstick—" She stopped. "Don't worry. We'll all stick together. We'll help you remember what to do."

Beast looked at Kissie.

He looked at Jill.

"Maybe," he said.

Matthew would feel like a million dollars.

"I'll ask Matthew if I can borrow his shirt," he said.

He galloped across the mall. He waved his hat. He felt just like Paul Revere.

He could do this play. He knew he could.

"The British are coming," he yelled. "But the good guys are going to win."

He felt like a million dollars.

The Polk Street Guide to Boston

The Polk Street Kids' Boston Favorites:
Places to Visit, Things to Do,
and Famous People
(listed in alphabetical order)

Ms. Rooney says:

Do you like baked beans? Boston is called Beantown.

Years ago, people thought it was wrong to cook on Sunday. They cooked beans on Saturday . . . and ate them the next day with brown bread.

And try a cup of clam chowder. Bostonians add milk or cream to it. They say it's thick enough when you can stand your spoon up in it.

Don't forget to have Boston cream pie for dessert. It's the best!

And now, put on your traveling shoes. We'll tell you what else we like about Boston.

Emily Arrow says:

Don't miss *Boston Common,* the oldest park in the country. It's a huge grassy spot. It's been there since the olden days. The colonists' cows and sheep grazed there. British soldiers marched there too.

Bordered by Boylston, Charles, Beacon, Park, and Tremont Streets

Jill Simon likes:

The *Public Garden.* It has a neat pond with a bridge. You can feed the ducks and ride on the swan boats. Read *Make Way for Ducklings* before you go. You'll see the bronze ducklings heading for the park.

Bordered by Charles, Beacon, Arlington, and Boylston Streets

Ms. Rooney says:

You might want to walk along part of the *Freedom Trail.* You can see many places that date from the American Revolution. The trail is about three miles long. The sidewalk is marked with painted red lines or bricks.

> Start at the Visitors Information Booth at the Common. Pick up a map that describes the places on the trail.

Beast says:

See the *Old Granary Burying Ground.* It's a place on the Freedom Trail. Paul Revere is buried there. So are some other important people: John Hancock, who

signed the Declaration of Independence, Elizabeth (Mother) Goose, and even Benjamin Franklin's mother and father.

Near the corner of Park and Tremont Streets

And Matthew Jackson wants you to know:

Another place on the Freedom Trail is the *Paul Revere House.* It was built in 1680. It's the oldest building in Boston. Some of the furniture is still in the house . . . and pieces of silver made by Paul Revere. A 931-pound metal bell that he made is outside.

19 North Square (between Richmond and Prince), (617) 523–2338

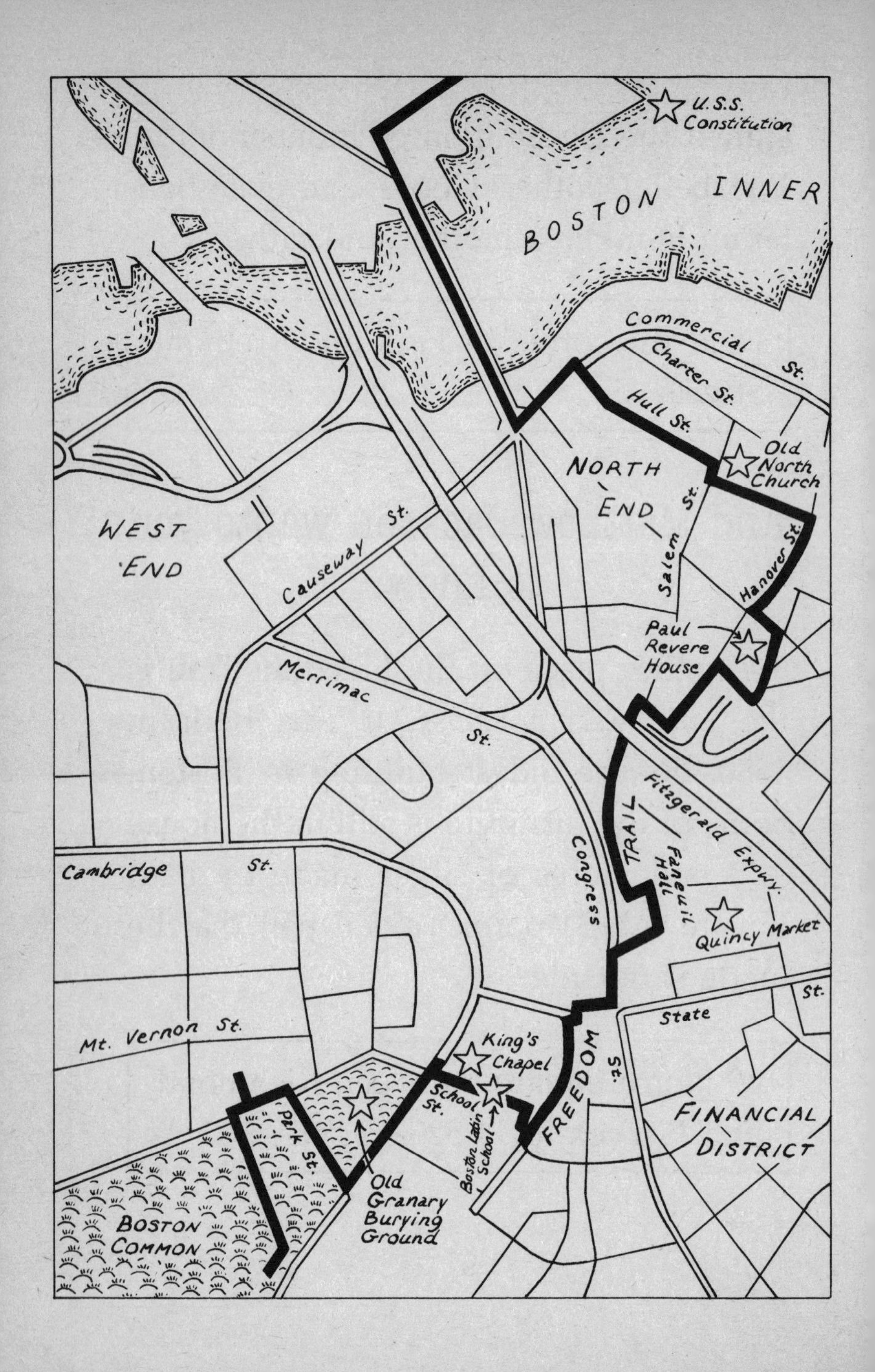
U.S.S. Constitution
BOSTON INNER
Commercial St.
Charter St.
Hull St.
Old North Church
NORTH END
Salem St.
Hanover St.
WEST END
Causeway St.
Paul Revere House
Merrimac St.
Fitzgerald Expwy.
TRAIL
Faneuil Hall
Congress
Quincy Market
Cambridge St.
State St.
Mt. Vernon St.
King's Chapel
School St.
FREEDOM
St.
FINANCIAL DISTRICT
Park St.
Boston Latin School
Old Granary Burying Ground
BOSTON COMMON

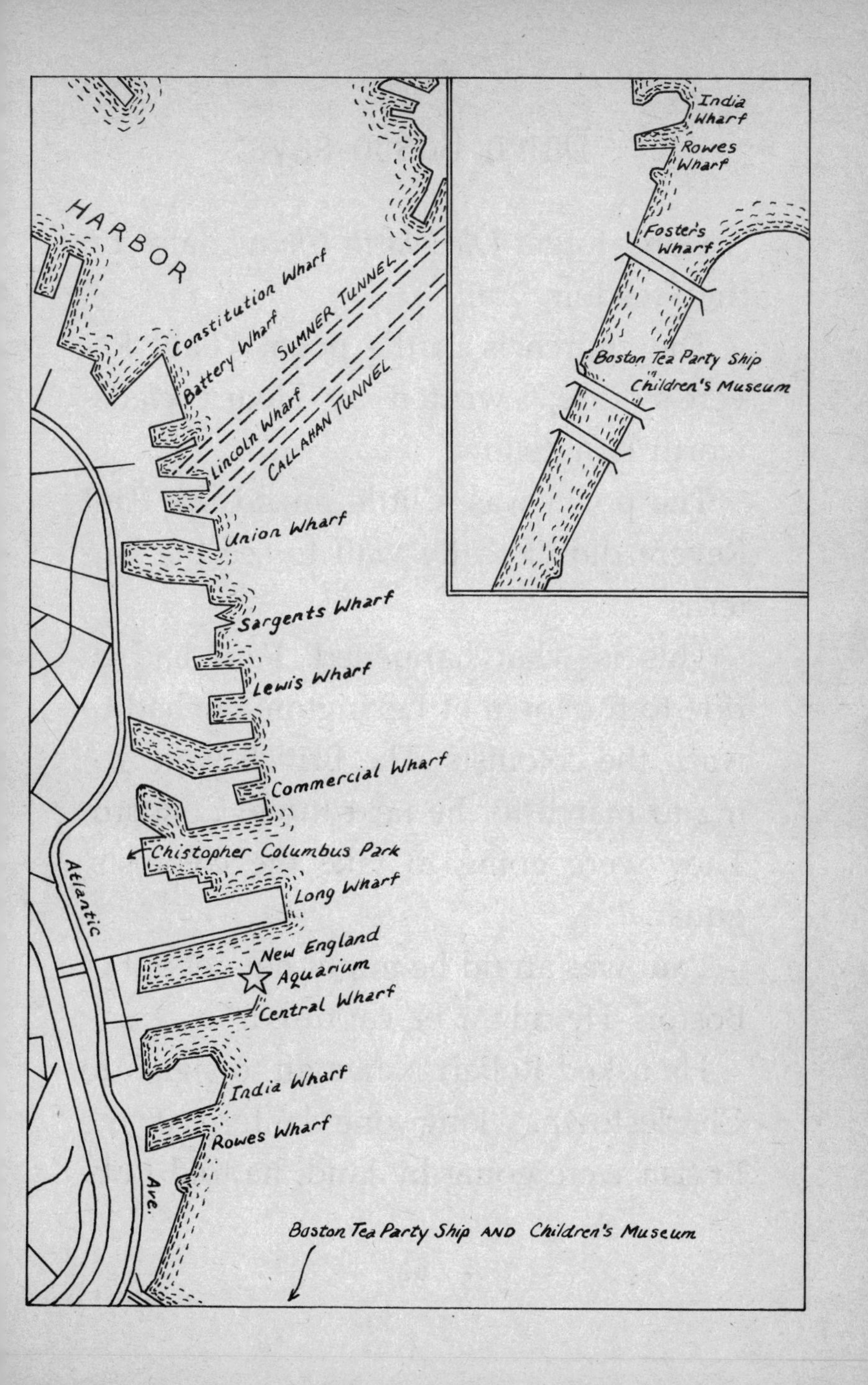
HARBOR
Constitution Wharf
Battery Wharf
SUMNER TUNNEL
Lincoln Wharf
CALLAHAN TUNNEL
Union Wharf
Sargents Wharf
Lewis Wharf
Commercial Wharf
Chistopher Columbus Park
Long Wharf
Atlantic
New England
Aquarium
Central Wharf
India Wharf
Rowes Wharf
Ave.
Boston Tea Party Ship AND Children's Museum
India
Wharf
Rowes
Wharf
Foster's
Wharf
Boston Tea Party Ship
Children's Museum

Dawn Bosco says:

Don't forget *Old North Church* (also on the Freedom Trail).

The church is in the poem "Paul Revere's Ride," written by Henry Wadsworth Longfellow.

The poem was a little mixed up. Paul Revere didn't really wait to see the lanterns.

This is what happened. Paul had to ride to the town of Lexington. He had to warn the colonists. The British were going to march to the next town, Concord. They were going to take the colonists' guns.

Paul was afraid he might not get out of Boston. He might be captured.

He asked Robert Newman to signal to Charlestown. Hang one lantern if the British were going by land, he told Robert. Hang two lanterns if they were going by boat across the Charles River.

Robert Newman watched. The British were going by boat.

He hung two lanterns.

You can look up at the tower. You'll see where it happened.

You can see other things at the church too. You can see twelve bricks from the Pilgrim days. The bricks were from William Brewster's prison cell in England.

193 Salem Street

Timothy Barbiero writes:

I like the *New England Aquarium.* It has a huge fish tank, three stories high. It's

the largest in the world. You'll see sharks and giant sea turtles. You can watch divers feeding them every day. Other things to see: dolphins, sea lion shows, and about seven thousand fish.

> Central Wharf at Milk Street,
> (617) 973–5200

Alex Walker says:

You might want to walk along the *Black Heritage Trail.* It's about a mile and a half long. You'll see houses, churches, and schools that have to do with black history.

> Information at the National Park Service Visitors Center, 15 State Street, or the Museum of Afro-American History, 46 Joy Street, (617) 742–1854

Jason Bazyk writes:

Take a look at the *John J. Smith House.* Smith was a black statesman. He owned

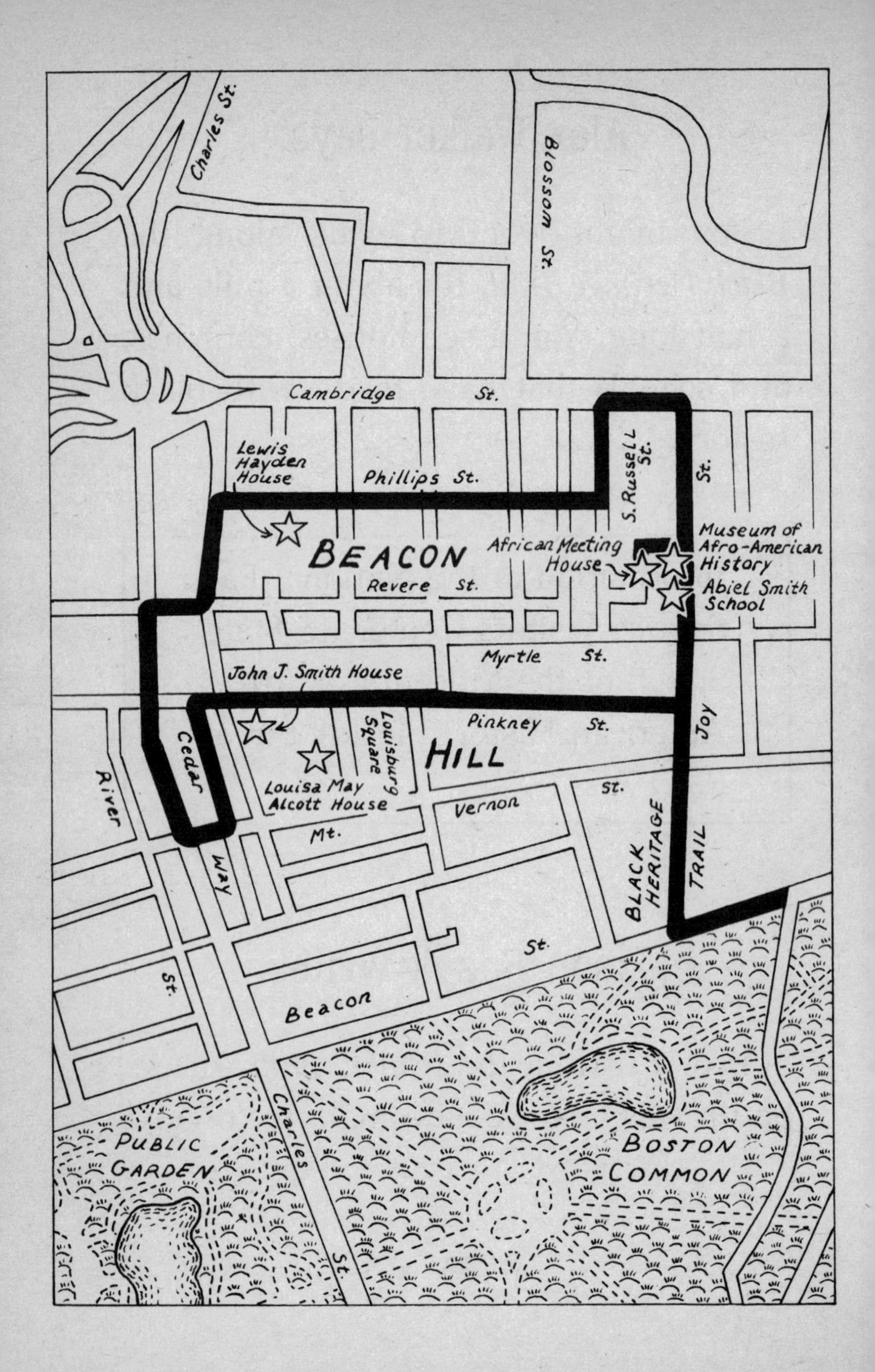
Charles St.
Blossom St.
Cambridge St.
Lewis Hayden House
Phillips St.
S. Russell St.
St.
African Meeting House
Museum of Afro-American History
Abiel Smith School
BEACON
Revere St.
Myrtle St.
John J. Smith House
Pinkney St.
Louisburg Square
Joy
Cedar
HILL
River
Louisa May Alcott House
Vernon
St.
Mt.
Way
BLACK HERITAGE
TRAIL
St.
St.
Beacon
PUBLIC GARDEN
Charles
St.
BOSTON COMMON

a barbershop that was a meeting place for runaway slaves.

86 Pinckney Street (on the Black Heritage Trail). The inside is not open to the public.

Noah Green says:

See the *Lewis and Harriet Hayden House.* Lewis Hayden was a slave who escaped through the Underground Railroad. His house became a stop on the railroad to help other runaway slaves.

66 Phillips Street (on the Black Heritage Trail). The inside is not open to the public.

Sherri Dent writes:

Go to the *Abiel Smith School.* It was built in 1834 for black students. Today it's a museum. You can learn about African American history.

46 Joy Street at Smith Court (on the Black Heritage Trail)

Matthew wants to tell you:

I like *Christopher Columbus Park.* Watch the boats in the harbor . . . and the planes zoom off from Logan Airport.

On the waterfront at Long Wharf

Derrick Grace says:

Don't miss *Fenway Park.* See the *Red Sox* play baseball. The left-field wall is really high. It's hard to hit home runs there. The wall is painted green. People call it the Green Monster. If you like basketball, see the *Boston Celtics.* They play at the *FleetCenter* from October through April.

Fenway Park: 4 Yawkey Way, (617) 267–8661; FleetCenter: Causeway Street, (617) 523–3030

Emily writes:

Wait until you see the giant milk bottle. You can have lunch inside. Then go into the *Boston Children's Museum.* You can touch almost everything, climb on sculptures, blow bubbles, and see a Japanese home. Dress up in Grandmother's Attic. Pet and hold a live lizard . . . and play computer games. Whew! There's a lot to do.

Museum Wharf, 300 Congress Street, (617) 426–8855

Sherri loves:

Faneuil Hall. It's called the Cradle of Liberty. You'll see it on the Freedom Trail. The colonists met here. Look up to see the grasshopper weather vane on top. It was made in 1742.

Quincy Market is right there. It faces *Faneuil Hall.* You'll love the food . . . bread and pizza and cookies and fruit

and everything. You'll love the gifts to buy. You'll love the magicians. You'll love the whole thing.

Dock Square, (617) 242–5642

Linda Lorca says:

How about *Charlestown Navy Yard*? It's on the *Freedom Trail*. This place is huge. You can see the USS *Constitution*. This ship's nickname is "Old Ironsides." It's the oldest commissioned warship in the world. It first sailed in 1797. It won twenty-four battles. Guess who made the sheathing, bolts, and fittings? Paul Revere! You can also see the USS *Cassin Young,* a World War II destroyer. Fleets from around the world dock here. Don't miss the playground facing Pier 4. There's a ship in the sand to climb on, and a wading pool.

Constitution Avenue, Charlestown, (617) 242–5601; USS *Constitution* information, (617) 242–5670

Jill writes:

It turned out that I liked *Franklin Park* after all. It's the largest park in the Emerald Necklace . . . and even though it's a ride from Boston, you might want to go to the Kite-Flying Festival. Thousands of

people send up their kites. It looks wonderful. The *Franklin Park Zoo* is there, with hippos, baboons, and other animals in a tropical forest. The *Children's Zoo* is there too. You can see baby animals and pet the goats and lambs.

Blue Hill Avenue and Columbia Road, Dorchester, (617) 442–2002

Pop tells the class:

See the *Boston Tea Party Ship and Museum.* You can throw boxes of tea into the harbor. The colonists did that two hundred years ago. They wanted to show the British they wouldn't pay a tax on tea. Have a cup of tea too.

Congress Street Bridge, off Atlantic Avenue, (617) 338–1773

Wayne O'Brien writes:

Don't forget to visit *Chinatown*. Look for the pagoda on top of the Chinese Merchants Building. Enjoy a moon cake or a golden fish cookie at a bakery. Walk over to the fish market. You'll see tanks of colorful fish.

> Chinatown is bounded by Kneeland, Washington, and Essey Streets and the Central Artery.

Dawn wants to tell you:

Outside the *F.A.O. Schwarz* toy store is a special bear. He's bronze and he weighs six thousand pounds. The bear was the toy store's gift to the children of

Boston. After you've seen the bear, go inside and shop for toys.

Corner of Berkeley and Boylston Streets, (617) 262–5900

Beast says:

The *Longfellow National Historic Site* was really neat. You might take a poetry workshop during Family Days in August . . . or take home a poetry-writing kit. Henry Longfellow lived here and wrote poetry for many years.

105 Brattle Street, Cambridge, (617) 876–4491

Jill says:

If I could play hopscotch, I'd go straight to School Street. Outside the *Old City Hall* is a wonderful hopscotch game. It tells the story of the *Boston Latin School*. That's America's first public school.

45 School Street

Jason writes:

I liked *Old South Meeting House.* It's a great museum. It tells about the Boston Tea Party and other things that happened in the Revolutionary War.

310 Washington Street, (617) 482–6439

Miss Kara, the art teacher, likes:

King's Chapel. What a beautiful church this is. Its bell was made by Paul Revere.

You'll see the pew George Washington used when he visited. The steeple isn't pointed. The church members didn't have enough money for that!

58 Tremont Street (corner of School Street), (617) 227–2155

Mrs. Miller, the Killer, the substitute teacher, says:

You'll love the *Boston Symphony Orchestra Youth Concerts.* There's a set in the fall, and one in the spring. Saturday sessions are for parents and children.

301 Massachusetts Avenue,
(617) 638–9375

Matthew writes:

Like to be up high? You can go to the *John Hancock Observatory,* on the sixtieth floor of the John Hancock Tower. Telescopes will give you an up-close view of the Boston sights.

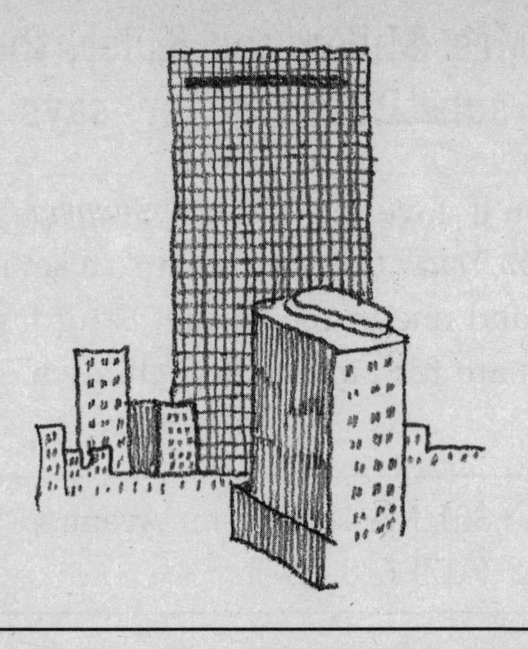

Hancock Place at Copley Square, (617) 247–1977

Dawn wants to tell you:

If you like to look up at the stars, see the *Hayden Planetarium*. You'll learn about the stars over Boston, black holes, and supernovas.

Science Park, (617) 723–2500

Miss Kara likes:

The *Museum of Fine Arts.* Drop into the Children's Room for a workshop. Take a

class using paint, paper, pencils, and other media.

465 Huntington Avenue, (617) 267–9300

Emily writes:

Did you read *Little Women,* by Louisa May Alcott? Louisa May Alcott lived and wrote here in Louisburg Square. (The house where she grew up and where she

wrote *Little Women* is in Concord. It's not far from Boston.)

No. 10 and No. 20 Louisburg Square

About the Author/About the Artist

Patricia Reilly Giff is the author of more than sixty books for young readers, including *Lily's Crossing,* a *Boston Globe–Horn Book* Fiction Honor Book, and these popular series: the Kids of the Polk Street School, the Lincoln Lions Marching Band, and the Polka Dot Private Eye. She lives in Weston, Connecticut.

Blanche Sims has illustrated all of the Polk Street books. She lives in Westport, Connecticut.